HANSON

An Unauthorized Biography

HANSON

An Unauthorized Biography

by
Michael-Anne Johns

SCHOLASTIC INC.

New York   Toronto   London   Auckland   Sydney

ISBN 0-590-10683-X

12 11 10 9 8 7   7 8 9/9 0 1 2/0

Printed in the U.S.A.

First Scholastic printing, September 1997

Photo credits:

front cover: Anja Grabert; **back cover:** Gregg DeGuire/London Features; **insert: p. 1** Anja Grabert; **p. 2** (all) Alan Singer; **p. 3** (all) Alan Singer; **p. 4** Anja Grabert; **p. 5** (all) Anja Grabert; **p. 6** Gregg DeGuire/London Features; **p. 7** Gregg DeGuire/London Features; **p. 8** Gregg DeGuire/London Features; **p. 9** Ernie Paniccioli; **p. 10** (top) Ernie Paniccioli/Retna Limited USA; (bottom) Ernie Paniccioli; **p. 11** (top) Jeffrey Mayer; (bottom) Gregg DeGuire/London Features; **p. 12** Jeffrey Mayer; **p. 13** Ernie Paniccioli/Retna Limited USA; **p. 14** Jeffrey Mayer; **p. 15** Jeffrey Mayer; **p. 16** Anja Grabert

Contents

HANSON

An Unauthorized Biography

"THINKING OF YOU"

"... Fly with wings of an eagle
Glide along with the wind
No matter how high
I'll be thinking of you the whole time . . . ."

Written by: Isaac Hanson/Taylor Hanson/Zachary Hanson
Producer: The Dust Brothers (John King and Michael Simpson)
Album: *Middle of Nowhere*
Length: (3:13)

FAST FACT: "We were just jammin' together and the song started flowing and in about thirty minutes it was written," recalls Isaac of the writing process of "Thinking of You." "That's a weird example of how a song can come together. It happens in all kinds of different ways."

1
Meet Hanson — Three Brothers Who Rock!

"Hanson is three brothers, and
we love making music."
Isaac Hanson

In the early spring of 1997 — March 24 to be exact — the infectious beat of "MMMBop" was first heard on the radio airwaves of America. Radio DJs introduced "MMMBop" with comments such as, "And, here, from the heartland of Oklahoma, is Hanson with their debut single, 'MMMBop'!"

As listeners everywhere tried to hear the lyrics, the question arose: WHO IS HANSON?

Well, the fans who were toe-tapping and singing along with "MMMBop" didn't have to wait too long to find out. MTV introduced the "MMMBop" video on May 6, 1997, and the world finally saw Hanson! They were three blond,

long-haired brothers from Tulsa, Oklahoma —
sixteen-year-old Isaac, fourteen-year-old Taylor,
and eleven-year-old Zachary.

The last time the pop music scene had stirred
such excitement was when five hip-hopping
boys from Boston got together as the New Kids
On The Block. After that, the grunge and alternative scene took over and kids were trading in
their baggy pants and unlaced sneakers for
oversized plaid flannel shirts and chunky shoes.

And then HANSON came along!

I Like Ike!

Clarke Isaac Hanson was born on November
17, 1980. He's the oldest of the Hanson siblings,
which in total includes brothers Taylor, Zachary,
Mackenzie, and sisters Jessica and Avery. He's
often been compared, in looks, to actor Stephen
Baldwin, the youngest brother of another tal-
ented family.

But who is this sixteen-year-old, guitar-play-
ing Hanson? What is he really like behind this
exterior? Well, first of all, the oldest Hanson sibling has often described himself as "goofy,"
"silly," "sometimes even stupid, but fun." He's
been known to keep his brothers laughing even
on long, boring trips in a tour bus or van. Isaac,
or Ike as he likes to be called, has a great sense
of humor, but there is a serious side behind that
smile, too.

Ike has been writing songs since he was eight years old. His parents, Diana and Walker, were always singing and playing music around the house, so Ike grew up with a special appreciation of it. Even today he sees music as a release, a way to express sorrow and joy. "There's every [kind of] hard stuff in life, plenty of stuff to get down about," he says. "For us, music is a way to get away from things."

Even though Ike is the oldest sibling, he isn't into laying down laws and pushing to get his way. Perhaps because the Hanson kids have all been home-schooled and spent so much time together, they've developed an almost second instinct about each other.

"Getting sick of each other, it's not an issue, because we're brothers and we enjoy each other's company," Ike observes. "We like to tease and fight all the time, but it's all in fun."

Even when they write songs together, they give each other space and respect. The process is simple, according to Ike: "[We write about] things that happen. We're inspired by all sorts of different things. Sometimes I'll just look out the window and something clicks."

Well, if you listen to *Middle of Nowhere*, you do hear a lot about love. So, what about the topic of girls when it comes to Ike? Has he ever been in love? Has he ever had his heart broken?

"We're allowed to date," Ike explains, "but

right now is probably not the time. For one thing, no girlfriend would probably want to deal with our schedule."

Even Ike realizes that at sixteen, he has a lot of time ahead of him for dating, hanging out with friends, and just relaxing. Right now he's willing to dedicate himself to music because for Hanson it's "what we do and the reason we do it is because we love it!"

Totally Taylor!

Next in line is Jordan Taylor Hanson. He was born on March 14, 1983, which makes him a Pisces. If you believe in astrology, Taylor is a perfect Pisces since it's the sign of those who are creative, spiritual, imaginative, and . . . musical. Pisces have a tendency to look deeply into subjects, to explore things, and to feel things others may not. In short, Pisces are sensitive people.

Though Taylor, whose nickname is Tay, has the spotlight most often since he is usually Hanson's lead singer, the attention has not gone to his head. No big ego here. As a matter of fact, Tay admits that he's a bit shy — especially when the girls start screaming his name. And, if you want to get on his good side, don't compare him to other musical greats — it embarrasses him.

Like his older brother, Tay is very serious

about music and establishing a long-term career. "We just really have to work at it," he says. "That's important, but you also have to realize that the focus is loving this music and that being the point of why we're doing it."

As for his relationship with his brothers, Tay says: "We're always hanging out — we're basically best friends."

And what about that other kind of friend? Girlfriends? Well, agreeing once more with Ike, Tay says, "None of us have girlfriends right now. We just don't have the time."

But he's not saying NEVER. As a matter of fact, Tay admits that if he met a perfect girl asking for his autograph or standing in line to buy a ticket to a Hanson show, he'd ask her out. Of course, he does have some qualifications. "If somebody's obsessed with you, it would be kind of hard to go out with her," he explains. "You'd take her hand and she'd scream! But if she was nice enough, then yeah, I'd date a fan."

Zac Attack!

Zachary Walker Hanson was born on October 22, 1985. Zac is known as the "maniac" of Hanson. He's a live wire whose fuse is always lit! He's the comic relief, the joker of the band, and his wild antics always encourage the fans to exercise their lung power — even though he always seems to be complaining that all the screaming is going to make him go deaf!

But Zac does admit that his high-energy ways could just be a cover up! "I think it's probably that I'm so shy that I just act wacky to make up [for it]."

If that's true, Zac is doing a great job of hiding his quiet side! Taylor shared a funny story about his little brother. Taylor said, "He's dragged people up onstage [during shows]. We would give T-shirts away. This one girl raised her hand, but she was too embarrassed to come up, so he went out there and carried her on the stage!"

How do Ike and Tay handle the Zac Attack? With love and understanding — and a good sense of humor. However, there is one time when he really can get on their nerves! Ike admits that like typical brothers, "We like to tease sometimes." But when it's onstage, that's something else. Tay explains: "Zac's the drummer, so he'll go, 'I'm the drummer, I'll do whatever I want.' So he'll speed us up, slow us down, whatever he wants to do." Music is no laughing matter for Isaac and Taylor.

Unfortunately for Zac, he has to come out from behind his drums sometime! But no matter how mad Ike and Tay may be, all Zac has to do is flash that gap-toothed grin, and they melt. They also don't let him forget he could be replaced — they do have a Hanson-in-training in little brother Mackie.

As a matter of fact, Zac half-seriously says: "Mackie's got the rhythm. I've got to watch out. He'll steal my place!"

As for the girls, well, Zac is definitely a typical eleven year old. One minute he's holding his hands over his ears complaining about the girls screaming his name and trying to grab at him, and the next he's flirting like a pro! He is in total agreement with his older brothers about it being hard to keep a steady relationship — especially when they were making *Middle of Nowhere*. "They'd only see us for one minute out of the year, because we live in Oklahoma and then we were in Los Angeles making an album and a video and then we're performing somewhere else!" he told *Teen Beat* magazine. And then there's the fact that his mom, Diana, would have something firm to say about an eleven year old having a girlfriend!

Family Values!

If Ike, Tay, and Zac are as down-to-earth as they seem — and they are — it's all because of their parents, Diana and Walker Hanson. They have always been there for their boys, encouraging them, and supporting them both financially and emotionally.

All three brothers in Hanson are very appreciative. Ike says, "Our parents have been really great about just supporting us in general. [They tell us] 'Guys, if you want to stop, we'll stop. If you want to keep going and push harder, let's push harder.' They've just been there to back us up."

And, oh, according to Zac, their parents have been important for one other reason — "Without them we couldn't drive to our shows!"

That Zac! But the fact is some outsiders may have the wrong impression of Diana and Walker, judging them to be stage parents.

Well, one old friend, Terry Grusik, does call them stage parents, "But not in a negative way. Not at all! They were just good self-promoters of their kids. They would take care of details."

And Tamra Davis, who directed both of Hanson's videos, "MMMBop" and "Where's the Love," was equally impressed with the family dynamics. "Their family is interesting and rare," she observes. "When you work with them, it's really amazing. Their mom and dad and other siblings were very much around. You really saw them as a really strong family unit. The thing that completely amazed me is that they don't criticize each other, they don't fight with each other. . . . It was unbelievable. These kids wouldn't make the others feel insecure; they actually support each other. They were so loving with each other. . . . I definitely credit their parents in raising them like that."

And, according to Tamra, the younger Hansons share that same sweetness, that same sensitivity. The whole family was on the sets of the videos. Tamra recalls: "Their little sisters, Jessie and Avey, kept bringing me drawings. They were [coloring] in the dressing room and they kept bringing me these precious little pictures. I have them on my wall here at home."

It's obvious from all who come in contact with this family from the heartland, their success is well-deserved!

"MMMBOP"

"You have so many relationships in this life
Only one or two will last. . . .
Then you turn your back and
they're gone so fast . . . ."

**Written by: Isaac Hanson/Taylor Hanson/Zachary
Hanson**
**Producer: The Dust Brothers (John King and
Michael Simpson)**
Album: *Middle of Nowhere*
Length: (4:28)
First Single/Video Release

FAST FACT: According to Isaac, "MMMBop" is "basically about friends . . ." and, adds Zac, ". . . holding on to the ones who really care." Taylor, who sings lead on "MMMBop," says this is his favorite song from *Middle of Nowhere*. He also explains that they chose three *M*'s for the word MMMBop because "it just looked good." Isaac continues: "Three *M*'s looks like the right size. It wasn't quite MMMMMBop, and it wasn't quite MMBop; it was MMMBop, a little bit in the middle. It just looked good — three *M*'s and a Bop."

2
Life on the Road

**"There was always singing going around
and music in our house. We just naturally
started writing songs."**
Taylor Hanson

Walker and Diana Hanson grew up in Tulsa, Oklahoma, and met when they attended Nathan Hale High School. They had a lot in common, and almost immediately became high school sweethearts. Walker and Diana were very active members of the student body, but their favorite extracurricular activity was theater. They appeared in many school musical productions, often in the lead roles.

Terry Grusik, who today is the program director of the Tulsa Performing Arts Center, recalls their school days fondly. "Walker and Diana were a couple of years behind me," Grusik says, "but I knew them. I met them through the theater department because I was a theater person, too. I remember, one year after I graduated, and before they were married, they both had the leads in *The King and I* production. Walker played the King and Diana was Anna."

When Walker and Diana went on to college, they continued pursuing their musical talents. Diana was a music major and she and Walker sang with a church group called The Horizons and performed across the country. Though gospel music was their main interest at the time, both loved to listen to rhythm and blues and rock and roll. Music was a very big part of their lives.

After college, Walker and Diana married and settled down in Tulsa to start a family and a new life. As a career, Walker was drawn to oil, Oklahoma's main industry. As the Hanson family grew with the births of Isaac in 1980, Taylor in 1983, and Zachary in 1985, Walker was climbing the ladder of success at Helmerich & Payne, Inc., an international oil drilling and gas exploration company. By 1989 he was H&P's Manager of International Administration. At that point, Walker's job took the Hanson family overseas. They lived in Ecuador, Venezuela, and Trinidad-Tobago — all major oil regions where H&P has drilling operations.

Hundreds of H&P families have been sent to

these exotic locations. Whether they live in a luxurious villa in Trinidad-Tobago or in the H&P camp in Venezuela, the families know they are definitely "not in Kansas anymore" — and in the Hansons' case, not in Oklahoma!

Man-sized iguanas, wild parakeets and parrots, lush jungles, and even sun-bathing crocodiles were part of the everyday scenery at the Venezuelan H&P camp. Of course, there were plenty of bats and rats, too. But according to one of Walker Hanson's co-workers, Marty Carley, it was the experience of a lifetime. As a matter of fact, Carley had spent three years in Venezuela when he was a kid when his father worked for H&P. Carley then returned ten years later with his own family. "Living in Venezuela is a great experience for a kid," Carley says. " What could be better than being able to swim every day of the year?"

Even though Walker and Diana wanted Isaac, Taylor, and Zachary to get the most out of the opportunity of living in Venezuela, they were concerned the kids might get homesick for the things they took for granted back in Tulsa. Life in Venezuela was *very* different from home — there were no cars, no TV. There was radio, but Taylor says, "We didn't listen to the radio because we didn't understand it." So Walker and Diana wanted to make sure the kids had a little bit of home with them — music.

"We lived abroad because of our dad's job," Isaac told a reporter from *Billboard* magazine. "We started in Ecuador and Venezuela and then moved to Trinidad-Tobago. We had music tapes that my parents had gotten from the Time/Life series. It was [1957-1969] rock 'n' roll. Otis Redding, Chuck Berry, Little Richard, Bobby Darin, Aretha Franklin, the Beach Boys, all these people. . . . We heard songs like 'Rockin' Robin,' 'Summertime Blues,' 'Splish Splash.' That's good music. We listened to that tape a ton. . . . That was the first stuff we really listened to that we were inspired by."

"There was always music in the house," Taylor recalls. "My mom's been singing around the house and listening to a lot of music since I can remember.

"Our parents really introduced us to music. . . . like, our mom really liked Billy Joel and she'd say, 'Here guys, listen to this.'"

So it wasn't so surprising that the three siblings started singing. As a matter of fact, Isaac says, "Singing is in our genes!"

"The boys started singing when we went overseas," Walker remembers. "At night I would get the guitar and play to them for a half an hour. We brought along the [Time/Life] cassettes since there was no television. They just learned the words and tunes."

It was just natural for the boys to sing together. But when the family returned to Tulsa in 1990, they had no idea that their singing would take them in a very new — and exciting — direction.

"WEIRD"

"... Isn't it strange how we all get a
little bit weird sometimes....
Reaching for a hand that can understand,
someone who feels the same...."

Written by: Isaac Hanson/Taylor Hanson/Zachary
  Hanson/Desmond Child
Produced by: Steve Lironi
Album: *Middle of Nowhere*
Length (4:02)

FAST FACT: "'Weird' was inspired by the word *weird*,"
explains Taylor. "We were trying to —"
   "— think of interesting ideas for a song," interrupts
Ike. "No one had ever written a song about the word
'weird,' but, yet, we use the word in our language so
much . . ."
   "We-e-e-i-r-d!" yells Zac!

3
Back in the Heartland

**"Our parents didn't push us into this.
This was our thing."**
Zachary Hanson

When the Hanson family returned to Oklahoma, they settled in a rural section of West Tulsa, just outside of the Tulsa city border. They moved into a brown, stone house, with plenty of outdoor space.

Though the family had returned to an American suburb, some things didn't change from their stay overseas. While they were out of the country, Diana Hanson had home-schooled her sons, and when they returned to Tulsa, she continued to do so. Ike, Taylor, and Zac enjoyed it. And, it did give them more time to enjoy other activities — like singing.

One night, after the family had finished their

dinner, they were sitting around the table talking and kidding around. Isaac and Taylor started singing and tried to recreate the fabulous harmonies they had heard on the Time/Life tapes. "We started doing two-part harmony," Isaac says. "But two-part harmony didn't really sound too right," interjects Zac. "So they needed a third person!"

That's when Zac joined in for three-part harmony. And from that point on, Isaac says, "Zac didn't have a choice. He was kind of stuck!"

When Walker and Diana heard their children's harmonic voices, they taught them to sing "Amen" after saying grace at the family dinner table. And soon the boys were improvising tunes on their own.

"We were always singing," recalls Taylor. "Our parents would go out and ask us to do the dishes, and when they'd come back we wouldn't have done the dishes, but we'd have written a song! We didn't think about it; it just happened."

Diana and Walker encouraged Isaac, Taylor, and Zac in their musical interest. They gave them piano lessons, and things just sort of grew from there. "Forming a group was just a very natural thing," says Taylor. "And then we just wanted to get in front of crowds."

At first they called themselves The Hanson Brothers, then The Hansons, and eventually Hanson. They sang *a capella* (without instrumental accompaniment) and sometimes they sang to music tracks. When Diana and Walker realized that singing was more than just a hobby for their sons, they had a family meeting. After discussing the pros and cons of the boys pursuing a professional singing career, the Hanson clan got serious!

One of their first appearances was an *a capella* concert at their father's office Christmas party in 1991. An eleven-year-old Isaac, an eight-year-old Taylor, and a six-year-old Zac, dressed in jeans, white T-shirts, black jackets, dark sunglasses, and slicked-back, *short* hair, entertained the employees of Helmerich & Payne. The two newest members of the Hanson family were also there, daughters Jessica, who was three, and Avery, who was one. The boys impressed their father's co-workers so much that there was a feature story about Hanson in the next issue of the company magazine, *Enterprise*. That was just the beginning!

Their mom, Diana, basically began acting as their agent, getting the boys bookings at local events, clubs, and parties. Walker took over the duties of manager (later on he even played the guitar as part of a backup band for Hanson!) and took care of business. The major break for Hanson was a local Tulsa festival called Mayfest, which is a month-long celebration of arts in the city. There are concerts, art exhibits, museum open houses, club performances, and special events throughout the entire month of May. In 1992, they were invited to participate in a Mayfest musical competition. "We started performing as a group . . . at a local festival," Isaac recalls. "We were actually doing *a capella* then."

The funny thing is that, though the group caused quite a stir when they performed at Mayfest, they didn't walk away the big winners.

Terry Grusik, the program director of the Tulsa Performing Arts Center, has been a Mayfest volunteer over the years. In 1992, he was asked to start an event to be called the Community Stage. "It was designed to feature amateur and professional talent from Tulsa and the surrounding communities," Grusik recalls. "Since we had never done it before, the first year we turned it into a talent contest. We had preliminary contests and weeded out acts until we had the top twenty-five. They would come back and perform on the final Saturday of Mayfest for prize money. That's where I first came across the brothers. They were great, but they didn't win that year."

Even though Hanson didn't walk away with the prize money, Walker remembers the thirty-minute show as having been sensational. They sang fifteen songs all together. And Walker recalls, "Isaac and Taylor also sang six songs they had written. They worked off each other and picked up the rhythm."

Grusik realized when he met with the Hansons during the competition, that the boys' parents, Diana and Walker, were his schoolmates from Nathan Hale High School! But it wasn't this personal connection that made Grusik keep an eye on the group that was at first described as a "little white boy hip-hop trio."

It was actually the fan base Hanson was establishing in the local area as they began to play more and more dates. Over the next five years, Hanson would make close to three hundred appearances throughout the Midwest. But no matter how popular they were becoming, they always went back and performed for Mayfest's Community Stage.

"After that first year I secured a base of talent so that I didn't need to have a contest anymore," Grusik says. "I just had these artists who would like to perform at the festival every year. Hanson performed for me every year from 1992 to 1996."

Hanson was really beginning to make a name for themselves. After the 1992 Mayfest, the group traveled around, even appearing in Branson, Missouri, the music mecca of the Midwest. One of their favorite venues was the Big Splash Water Park in Tulsa, which has Family Nights during their summer season. Musical entertainment is a feature during these nights, and Hanson made their first appearance there in 1992. One of the managers of Big Splash, Becky Thomas, remembers the first time she heard of Hanson. "Diana called and said she would like the boys to play at the park," Thomas says. "She was very persistent."

Diana's determination worked, because after that first appearance Hanson returned to Big Splash a number of times over the next four years. Thomas recalls that the crowds grew larger and more devoted each time. That wasn't surprising since Diana had started a Hanson newsletter, and a local fan club had been established. Whenever Hanson was appearing locally, mailers were sent out and their Tulsa fans followed!

Becky Thomas also remembers that the boys were *equally* devoted to their fans. "They did their show," she says. "They were very polite and afterwards they signed autographs for all their fans. Only then did they get to go and swim and enjoy the park. But they did not try to run and go play or be snobby — they were very courteous to everyone."

Singing was definitely turning out to be something major for the Hanson family. After several years of constant work, Walker and Diana hired full-time managers — Christopher Sabec and Stirling McIlwaine. Taylor recalls how they first met and sang for Sabec on the street! "It was at the South By Southwest Music Conference in Austin, Texas," Taylor explains. "We were doing our little song and dance, *a capella*, and we said, 'We can sing for you.' We had our boom box — this was before we picked up instruments — and we sang. We also had a track of a song we had written, so we sang and danced to that, and that was how we met them."

Sabec remembers the meeting very well, too. "After they sang *a capella* for me, I just said, 'Where are your parents? I need to talk to them fast!'"

Then, in 1995, Ike, Taylor, and Zac were ready to take the next step. They had all taken piano lessons, but Isaac says, "We were very interested in other instruments. We wanted to make our own music instead of singing to a background track all the time."

So they decided that they would each pick an instrument. "A friend had a set of drums in his attic," Ike explains, "and then we went to a pawn shop and got a guitar."

And how did they decide who would play what instrument? Well, Taylor says he picked keyboards because, "I had already been playing keyboards — I had taken lessons." Ike picked the guitar, because, "Playing guitar gives you a whole different inspiration than the keyboard, and we needed that different inspiration." And Zac? Well, he has his own take on the subject, "I'm not that great a drummer, but everybody says I can play, so I'll take their word for it. The secret is, nobody else's arms are as long. I couldn't play the guitar or piano, so I went to the drums because I've got long arms."

Within one week of picking up their instruments, Hanson played live! "When we started playing, we weren't doing very much though," says Zac. "Just simple stuff, bang, bang, bang."

That soon changed and the boys became very proficient on their instruments. And, as the boys got better and better, Walker, Diana, and their new managers decided to go one step further — to the recording studios. However, it wasn't an easy leap. Christopher Sabec reveals that twelve record labels turned down Hanson during this time. "Most labels advised me to get away from this act as fast as possible," he confessed to a reporter for the British magazine *OutMusic*. "People said this act would ruin and humiliate me. It was very difficult."

Instead of being set back, Sabec, McIlwaine, Diana, Walker, and the boys took matters into their own hands. By 1995 the boys had written over one hundred songs of their own, so the family scraped together enough money to independently record and release a debut CD called *Boomerang*. There were nine songs on it, five of which they wrote. The cover songs included some of their favorites such as "Poison Ivy" and the Jackson 5's "The Love You Save." In 1996 they released their second independent CD, *MMMBop*. "We went into a garage studio with a guy and recorded our next album, *MMMBop*," Ike says. "We produced it ourselves and played all the instruments on it."

That CD, of course, included the single "MMMBop," but this version was slower and less jazzy than the one on the Mercury Records' release *Middle of Nowhere*.

As a matter of fact, Lewis Drapp, the owner of Drapp Studios in Tulsa, remembers that first "MMMBop" very well. Hanson recorded their second independent CD, *MMMBop* at his studio — and Drapp played on a number of the fifteen songs that were included in the CD.

Lewis Drapp has taught music and has even managed a music store. In 1991, he built an addition onto his home in Tulsa and set up a professional recording studio. "I work with a lot of individuals who don't know how to go about getting a recording done and they come to me," he says. "It's a neat business."

Drapp only lives four or five miles from the

Hansons, and once Walker and Diana checked out his studio, they knew it was for them. It was impressive and homey at the same time, and definitely reflected Drapp's musical knowledge.

"You walk in and it doesn't look like a home once you get inside," Drapp explains. "It's like a guitar museum. I've got just all kinds of weird instruments, from guitars, like, from Africa — just turtle shells with strings on them — to real nice antique guitars and banjos. We set it up with a cool atmosphere — everybody likes just coming here to gaze at everything. It's not like white walls."

At first Walker and Diana went along to the studio with Ike, Tay, and Zac, but after several visits, they felt comfortable dropping them off and picking them up later that day. "It wasn't a hassle," recalls Drapp, who has two youngsters of his own. "They're fun kids, [but] they know how to work and then when it's time to play."

The boys brought along their first CD, *Boomerang*, for Drapp to listen to and get a feel for their music. But they made one thing very clear about the project they were working on. "We want this one to be us," they told Drapp.

And it was. "They played the keyboards, guitar, drums, and I played the bass for them," Drapp says. "They wrote every song on it too. I was surprised. You know, they're still kids and learning, but as far as bands [I've seen over the years], they are just gifted, just exceptional. When you see them, it's not just your average guitar player and keyboard player, and whatever, who's just learning to play. They've got that extra gift that makes them excel."

Of course, it wasn't all work and no play. There were times they just had to take breaks and relax. Especially little Zac. After all, he was only nine years old at the time!

Drapp remembers the telltale sign that a break was needed. "After recording for a couple of hours, the little drummer would get real tired. He played great and then, like, all of sudden, he'd start playing quieter. And I'm like, where'd the snare go? He'd still be hitting it, but at different levels because he was getting tired! Drumming takes a lot of energy anyway, and then at his age, well, that's hard on a kid."

So that's when Ike, Taylor, and Zac would turn back into those "normal" Hanson kids. They would order pizza in and just kick back. Drapp recalls there was also time for other activities. "They'd bring some toys with them and play. Game-Boy type things and some Transformers — at least the little one, not the big ones. They would bring pencils and paper. They all loved to draw and do their own little thing for a while. . . . The cool thing about the CD they did here was when you opened up the cover, there was a two-page folder inside and it was all artwork done by them. A lot of character faces — funny ones, with real big mouths and real small noses. I think it was Taylor who liked to draw intricate things, like dinosaurs. The folder had dinosaurs, pictures of their band, a drum set, a picture of a guy with all these muscles riding a motorcycle. As a matter of fact, the kids created the Hanson logo."

But when it was time to get back to work, the pizza boxes were thrown out and the toys were put away. According to Drapp, it was usually Taylor who encouraged everyone to get back to work. "Taylor was the one who kept things going, sort of like his dad would if he were there," observes Drapp.

"Isaac is funny, he likes to do cartoon character voices," Drapp says. "We'd be in the middle of recording and he'd just start talking in a character voice and everybody would just fall apart laughing. He's a big cutup!

"On one song, we got so carried away with it; they actually meant to do character voices on it and we started kinda funnin'. I started goofing back with them, talking like Donald Duck, saying 'Hey, that's really cool.' So they made me get in there and do Donald Duck on one of their songs. I know we finished [the song], but I'm not sure if that one made it on the CD."

As for Zac, well Drapp remembers him as the biggest jokester. "He's very outgoing — on the spur of the moment," Drapp explains. "He's the one who'll just be quiet and then just cuts up, you know. He just has fun."

It was definitely a creative period for Ike, Tay, and Zac. Drapp recalls another time, the boys wanted to get the sound effect of a voice on the radio, so they ran home and got their walkie-talkies and recorded through them. Over a period of a couple of months, Ike, Tay, and Zac worked with Drapp to create *MMMBop*. They were determined to show the public just who Hanson really was!

When Hanson would appear at gigs, they would set up shop. They would bring out their autographed photos, their newsletters, their CDs and sell them right then and there. Hanson had definitely become a very successful little industry!

Hanson was so successful that they were constantly playing to overflow audiences. Take, for example, Hanson's memorable performance at Tulsa's Blue Rose Cafe. It was in the summer of 1996 and Ike says it turned into a major event. "The Blue Rose Cafe is a bar owned by a friend of ours. He really liked the music and wanted us to play there. But because it was a bar [and we were underage], we couldn't play inside. There's a really large wooden deck outside the cafe — basically half the people sit outside. So, during the summer a lot of people are out there —"

Taylor interrupts. "The point is, we had to play outside, but it ended up being better because the people from surrounding restaurants could come over. . . . That was the last concert we did before we made *Middle of Nowhere*."

Their hard work was starting to pay off, and it was only the beginning. As Walker Hanson looked back over the past few years, he told one reporter, "I never dreamed it would lead to this!"

"SPEECHLESS"

**"... The way you walk around me.
The way you talk around me.
You act so speechless. You've got
nothing to say...."**

**Written by: Isaac Hanson/Taylor Hanson/Zachary
 Hanson/Steve Lironi**
Producer: Steve Lironi
Album: *Middle of Nowhere*
Length: (4:20)

FAST FACT: This bouncy bit of heartbreak mourns the
last days of a romance gone bad. Taylor sings lead and
makes you believe he has been hurt by love before. It
can't be!

HANSON—ISAAC (16), TAYLOR (13), AND ZAC (11) —ON TOP OF THE CHARTS.

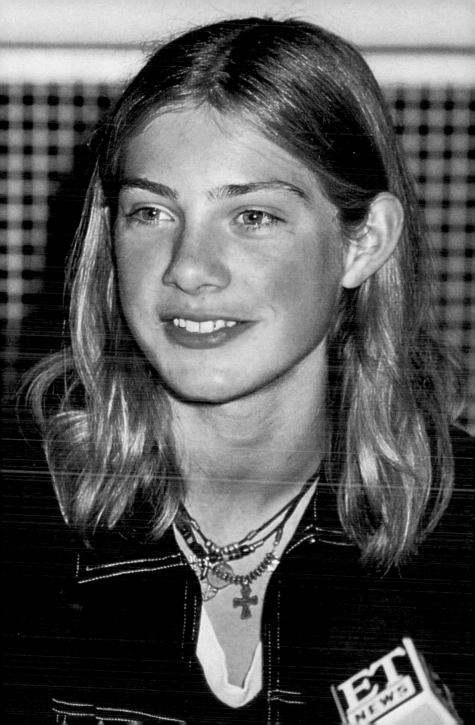

4
Sign on the Dotted Line

"People are coming back to music that's fun and upbeat, and younger artists are filling that gap."
Patti Galluzzi, MTV VP of Music & Talent

Hanson's *MMMBop* CD was released in May of 1996. Two months later the group did a show in Koffeeville, Kansas. It just so happened that Christopher Sabec, Hanson's manager, had sent a copy of *MMMBop* to Steve Greenberg, Vice President of A&R (Artists and Repertoire) at Mercury Records. After hearing the Hanson tape, the record company executive decided to check the group out.

"I was amazed that they completely recreated the music on their tape live," said Greenberg of his reaction after hearing Hanson play live. "They sang as well as they sang on the record, and played as well as they played on the record, and I was surprised on both counts. I had liked their tape, but I was convinced that it wasn't for real. . . . I was sure there was some adult pulling the strings or the vocals were manipulated and they weren't really playing their instruments. I wasn't going to [sign them]. But then I saw them at a county fair in Kansas. . . . There wasn't an adult in sight — except their dad, who was loading up the equipment, and their mom, who was selling T-shirts."

Seeing was believing for Greenberg and he immediately signed Hanson and brought them to L.A. to work on their first major label album. "They'd already written 'MMMBop,' their first great song, when we signed them," the record executive says. "But I felt they needed a lot of mentoring. They needed to be around a lot of people who could really help them make the right kind of record."

That's where Steve Lironi, who worked with Black Grape, the Dust Brothers, and Mark Hudson came into the picture. Greenberg had been impressed with Black Grape's CD *It's Great When You're Straight. . . Yeah!* "It was one of the best arranged records I've heard in a long time," he says, "so I suggested Steve Lironi. The guys needed help with arrangements. That was the most important thing."

The Dust Brothers, John King and Michael

Simpson, had produced Beck's multi-platinum album, *Odelay*, so Greenberg pulled them into the Hanson project, too. Hanson now had some great people on their team.

Isaac, Taylor, and Zac got down to work. They actually recorded *Middle of Nowhere* at the Dust Brothers' home studio. And part of their "MMMBop" video was filmed there, too.

"The Dust Brothers were really cool to work with," says Isaac. "The whole vibe of the studio was very laid-back. We'd come to the studio about noon and sit down and talk a little while, and when we felt like starting, we would. And they have a great record collection, obviously, 'cause they use a lot of different sampled things. So they'd play us different records — Three Dog Night, the Pointer Sisters, the entire Beatles' collection. It was really cool."

It was important to Hanson, as well as to the people from Mercury, that whoever the group worked with would keep the boys' original sound while polishing it just a bit. Greenberg explains what he sees as Hanson's appeal. "They write their own songs, they play their own instruments, sing great, and they have a vision. . . . Kids want that genuineness. They don't want a manufactured sound."

Isaac feels the Dust Brothers understood that exactly. They didn't change Hanson's sound, "But they added some interesting elements that

41

we might not have thought of," he says. "'MMM-Bop' is a good example. They added a 'ruh-uh-ruh-uh-ruh-uh' scratch thing."

Taylor agrees with his older brother. "I think what the Dust Brothers and Steve Lironi kinda brought back to our sound was a little of the R&B — with the loops and scratches and samples sounds — and combined it with pop rock."

Steve Greenberg also pulled in songwriter Mark Hudson to the project. Mark first came to the public's notice when he performed back in the 1970s with his brothers, Bill and Brett, as The Hudson Brothers.

Hudson was familiar with the pros and cons of working with a family group. And he was totally taken with Ike, Taylor, and Zac. The first time he met with them, Hudson recalls, "They brought guitars and ideas! They are adorable. I saw blonder versions of my brothers and myself. . . .It was like working with my brothers all over again."

Hudson, who has most recently been working with superstar groups such as Aerosmith and Bon Jovi, was impressed by the professionalism of Ike, Taylor, and Zac. As they worked together in his studio, he really got to know them. Between takes, they would all sit around — with Diana, Walker, Jessie, Avey, and the youngest addition to the Hanson family, Mackie — and just talk. They'd talk about everything from Power Rangers — Zac's favorite subject — to what to expect from the music industry and fans.

Hudson was already impressed at how the brothers were able to collaborate with someone like him, who was really a total stranger. Yet, they weren't so blown away by his credentials that they gave up on an idea they really believed in. Hudson told them if they expected to make it and still have integrity, there might be times when they would have to *fight* to make good music.

Mark Hudson also had advice on dealing with the fan frenzy. Isaac, Taylor, and Zac knew the Hudson Brothers music and realized Mark Hudson and his brothers had faced screaming crowds at one time too.

Hudson's advice was to keep everything in perspective, to rely on the love and family roots they have always had — even if one of the boys becomes more popular than the others. "Just remember to love each other," he said.

It took six months in L.A. for Hanson to record *Middle of Nowhere*, so once again the family picked up their Tulsa roots and relocated. They rented a house in the Hollywood Hills, and the three oldest brothers just concentrated on work, work, work. As 1996 turned to 1997, Hanson was finally on the verge of breaking out. By the end of January 1997, *Middle of Nowhere* was finished, and the master tape was already in production to spill out thousands, hopefully, millions, of CDs. "MMMBop" was scheduled as the first single to be released on March 24. So, at the end of February, Ike, Taylor, and Zac were ready to make the "MMMBop" video.

Thirty-year-old film and music video director Tamra Davis was tapped by Mercury Records to direct the video. Actually, it was *Davis,* who selected Hanson's "MMMBop" as her next project after Mercury sent her several tapes of new artists who needed videos.

Davis recalls, "I had just finished a movie and wanted to do a video because I hadn't done one for a year. I had worked with Mercury before and they sent me tapes from several groups. When I saw Hanson's picture and how cute they were and then heard 'MMMBop,' I was ready to go. I really liked their music — it was different. It was pop, but they looked like they were going to sound like Nirvana, like a rock band. But when I first heard their music, they sounded more like the Jackson 5. I thought they were really wonderful."

Davis is no stranger to directing videos — she has directed over 150! And she couldn't wait to get started on Hanson's. Davis says she immediately began coming up with ideas for the video. "At the time I was watching the history of NASA [on television] and all this stuff about the moon. But then I thought, they are eleven to sixteen years old, maybe I shouldn't be putting my ideas onto kids, that they probably had their own ideas. I felt it was really important to get their creative input."

Her sensitive attitude was definitely appreciated by the boys. "What was really cool about [Tamra] was she really wanted to know what we thought," says Taylor. "She called us before she told anybody else about her ideas for the video."

"When I talked to them," Davis continues, "it was really interesting because the first thing they said was they wanted to jump on the moon! It was really great!"

It's obvious that Tamra Davis, like so many others, quickly fell under the Hanson spell. Not only was she impressed with their talent, their family, their intelligence, but she became very protective of them, too. She realized that if "MMMBop" and *Middle of Nowhere* really exploded, they would be facing unknown territory. She wanted, in her own way, to help prepare them for that possibility. "I find if you keep [artists] creatively involved, it's exciting for them and they get a lot out of the work process," she explains. "And, for them being so young, it's important for them to feel they have some kind of control of who they are. A lot of that is the visualization of them and how they come off in 'MMMBop.'"

Davis and the boys sat down and tossed ideas back and forth. "A lot of 'MMMBop' came from them," says Davis. "Then it was up to me to figure out how to make it look good and make it look right."

Ike has good memories of those video days and the time spent planning with Davis. "She was very inclusive and there was a lot of creative input on both our parts," he says. "It was very much a collaborative effort."

During the discussions of what the boys wanted the "feel" of "MMMBop" to be, Davis says, "They said the song was kind of time travel — 'You're here and then you're there.' They told me they wanted it to look like *Honey I Shrunk the Kids*! They said, 'We want it to look like we're playing inside a flower.'"

And that is exactly the feeling "MMMBop" has! "It's just a fun video," says Taylor. "There's a lot of running around. And there's a part where we sing, 'Plant a seed/plant a flower/plant a rose,' and we throw some seeds down and a flower grows. We end up playing as a band on top of the flower. And then we're bouncing on the moon. And then we're with Einstein."

"MMMBop" took several days to film. They

were on location in the Dust Brothers' living room and on an isolated Malibu beach.

"I think the video really reflects who they are," Davis says. This became most obvious when the boys told her they weren't crazy about one of her suggestions. "When they leave the house, I wanted them to ride bicycles to get to the park. I wanted cool Schwinns — low-riders bikes. But they didn't want to do it. I didn't want to make a big deal of it, so I asked them how they wanted to get there. They were like: 'Let's take a cab, and then a bus, and then. . . . !' They didn't want to ride bicycles because they thought it would make them look too young! They thought taking a cab would make them look older!"

So, taking the lead from Ike, Taylor, and Zac, Davis played the sequence by ear. They didn't prearrange the cab; they just called for one and jumped in. They didn't get a permit to film on the bus; they just did it. And, as a result, you can actually feel the fun they were having.

All too soon the shoot for "MMMBop" was over, edited, and in the can, waiting to be released to MTV. But first, the powers-that-be at Mercury had a whole game plan ready to introduce these three brothers from Tulsa. It started on March 24, 1997, when the "MMMBop" single was released for radio airplay. That was a Monday. By the following Saturday, radio stations all across the country were getting phone calls from listeners asking, "Who is this Hanson?"

Mercury records wanted to introduce the hot new trio in a special way. Soon everyone would know about Hanson.

"WHERE'S THE LOVE"

**"Something has been going on and
I don't know what it is.
You don't mind the taking girl, but you
don't know how to give. . . ."**

**Written by: Isaac Hanson/Taylor Hanson/Zachary
Hanson/Mark Hudson/Sander Salover
Producer: Steve Lironi
Album: *Middle of Nowhere*
Length: (4:12)
Second Single/Video Release**

FAST FACT: Taylor sings the lead on this catchy love
song, "Where's the Love," and Isaac has a small solo about
the moment when you realize that love isn't always
enough to keep a relationship going. The video was filmed
on location in London and directed by Tamra Davis, who
also worked with them on "MMMBop." She was thrilled to
work with Hanson once more and described "Where's the
Love" as "crisper, not as rough-edged as 'MMMBop.' It has
to do with the world and what makes things turn in the
world, like love. It's really good."

5
That Was the Week That Was

"All these screaming girls and guys going crazy, you just have fun with it."
Taylor Hanson

As "MMMBop" entered *Billboard*'s charts at sixteen and began its climb to number one, Ike, Tay, and Zac were getting ready for the big push: the release of their CD, *Middle of Nowhere*. It was due to hit the stores on May 6, 1997, so the Mercury Records publicity machine went into overdrive as the date neared. Arrangements were made for the Hanson clan to take on New York City and to meet-and-greet what seemed to be *everyone*! That included TV appearances, photo shoots, magazine interviews, autograph signings, and mall performances.

The Hanson blitz began on May 5, 1997, with

an appearance on *The Rosie O'Donnell Show.* This was actually their national TV debut. When they joined Rosie on stage and Zac plopped himself down, swinging one leg over the arm of his chair, you knew it was going to be fun.

Rosie immediately gushed, "You guys, can I say something? You're awful cute! You're like a TV series waiting to happen."

Next Rosie compared them to the 1970s TV series *The Partridge Family*, but Ike admitted they had only seen reruns of the show because, "We're kinda, a little young."

"Yeah, you're young," Rosie giggled back in response to their ages. "Okay, don't rub it in!"

When Hanson performed with a three-man backup band, the audience got right into it and clapped along. By the time they sat back down and talked with Rosie some more, she couldn't say enough nice things about them! She even promised she'd come to their New York concert when they started their fall tour, and Ike assured her, "We'll have a backstage pass reserved for you, definitely!"

Rosie looked as if she had become a die-hard Hanson fan. She closed their segment with, "They're three brothers and they're a band. . . . They're so cutie patootie! Hanson is the name. I know you're gonna hear a lot from them!"

Hanson was off to a good start!

Their next big TV appearance was on *The Late Show with David Letterman* — it was May 6, the same day *Middle of Nowhere* hit the record stores. They performed, and Letterman came over to thank them.

Hanson was really looking forward to their next scheduled appearance on May 7, because it was going to be a performance in front of fans. Ike, Tay, and Zac — along with their family, backup band, and record company representatives — jumped into limos and sped through the Holland Tunnel to New Jersey and headed for the Paramus Park Mall. They were supposed to play at 8:00 P.M., but by 7:00 the entire court area of the mall was filled with frenzied fans. Some dedicated fans had been there since 1:30 in the afternoon, chanting "Hanson, Hanson, Hanson!" or singing "MMMBop" and holding signs saying, "I love you Taylor!" and "Zac! Come home with me!" and "I like Ike!" Girls even wrote their favorite Hanson's name on their foreheads in lipstick and markers!

The mall security force was very nervous — they had never seen anything like this. When the final count of fans was estimated, it was near the 4,000 mark! Girls were climbing up from the lower level to the top level where Hanson was going to play. When the boys finally arrived, it took them *forty-five minutes* just to get from the lower level to the makeshift stage that was set up.

The roar from the crowd was deafening and even Zac was shocked. At one point, the little guy yelled out, "Could you all be quiet! You're hurting my ears. Keep it down girls, I'm going to lose my hearing! Keep it down!"

Needless to say, that didn't work. You could barely hear the three songs they played. There was a short Q&A, where most of the questions centered around "Do you have girlfriends?"

With the mall security going into overtime and getting fearful of an out-and-out surge of "tween" girls, the Hanson appearance was cut short and Ike, Tay, and Zac were whisked away back to the Big Apple. But Paramus Park Mall wasn't the end of "the week that was!" Not by a long shot. There were numerous radio interviews and talk-fests with magazine editors and writers. There was an appearance on *CBS This Morning* in which host Mark McEwen predicted, "You're gonna be talking about [*Middle of Nowhere*] all year long. You're gonna hear it all summer long. 'MMMBop'. . . Hanson!"

In between appearances there were several major photo shoots — one with *Seventeen* magazine and another with *Interview* magazine. During the *Seventeen* photo shoot, which took place in New York City's Central Park, MTV caught up with Hanson. Ike, Tay, and Zac told the interviewer why they thought people were ready for Hanson. "Things change," Tay said. "They're always going to change." And Ike continued with, "I think music is always evolving. Things are always changing. People are always changing what they like. . . . like styles change, music changes."

As for trying to fit in with the alternative music scene that was riding the top of the charts when they first started making music, Ike explained, "We were always doing what we loved to do. We weren't worrying about what other bands were doing. We do what we do. And they do what they do. That's the way of the world."

They also confessed they hoped to *really* celebrate the success of "MMMBop" with those closest to them. "We're probably going to have a giant party with our friends . . . We'll definitely celebrate," Ike predicted. "Jump up and down!" laughed Taylor. "Get girlfriends!" Zac piped in, then in a more realistic moment he said, "Go to LaserQuest and play, like fifty times!"

The tone of the interview was set when the MTV reporter remarked to Zac that he was "the ham of the group." He immediately snapped back, "No. I'm the chicken!"

And, for a final bit of insight on Hanson, the MTV interviewer asked how they decided who would play each instrument in the group. Ike deferred to the youngest member of Hanson: "Zac has a philosophy [on] that one."

"Yeah, well the philosophy is . . ." Zac began. "My philosophy is, okay, nobody's arms were long enough [to play the drums]. So Ike [could] play the guitar. . . . the piano — [Tay] can play as well as [Ike]. . . ."

"So I went to the keyboard," Tay interjected.

"What else was left?" Zac asked rhetorically.

"Zac was left with the drums," Ike sums up the tale. "He kinda draws it out. He should tell it faster."

During their New York stay, Ike, Tay, and Zac did even more than many people knew. Besides their live appearances, they taped a number of TV shows that would be aired later in the month. One of these was an appearance on *Live With Regis & Kathie Lee*, which eventually ran on May 26. Kathie Lee, who is familiar with Hanson's hometown of Tulsa because she attended Oral Roberts University there, asked them about a recent honor: Hanson Day in Oklahoma.

Kathie Lee began, "Governor Frank Keating [declared it] . . ."

"Hanson Day," Regis finished, then asked, "Were you nervous about meeting the governor?"

Together Tay and Zac answered, "Actually we

didn't [meet him], because we were here [to do *Letterman*]!"

"They were on *Letterman;* they didn't have time to meet the governor!" joked Kathie Lee.

The New York leg of Hanson's debut week was drawing to a close, but there was definitely more in store for them — in Los Angeles. As Ike, Tay, and Zac settled down in their seats on the plane headed to California, they were still wound up — not only from all the excitement of the past days in New York, but in anticipation of the next day's event: an in-store appearance at Universal City Walk's Sam Goody record store.

The Los Angeles fans started lining up at 9:00 A.M. so they could be up front for Hanson's scheduled 1:00 P.M. appearance. *Los Angeles Times* reporter Robert Stevens was there and this is how he started his article about the Sam Goody show: "Eardrum-piercing, glass-shattering, banshees-have-nothing-on-us screams! The fans, primarily teenage girls, screamed when they glimpsed members of the adolescent trio waving from the balconies. They screamed before brothers Isaac, sixteen, Taylor, fourteen, and Zac, eleven . . . came onto the temporary stage erected downstairs. They screamed between the songs performed by the group at this free promotional concert, and they occasionally screamed during them. At times, they screamed for no reason at all."

Some 1,500 strong, the Hanson fans waited not-so-patiently as the boys did some interviews before they took the stage and performed four songs. By the last song, the decibel level was almost frightening, but Taylor ignored Zac's pleas for "quiet" and encouraged the crowd to scream as loudly as they could. They did, and the windows of the mall stores began to vibrate!

But that wasn't the end of it. With almost no sleep, Hanson returned to the airport the next day and flew back to New York for a May 12 in-concert appearance on NBC's *The Today Show*. As part of *The Today Show*'s summer concerts, Hanson played live outside the NBC Rockefeller Center offices. They rehearsed their harmonies *a capella*, snapping their fingers to the beat of the songs. Katie Couric came out and did a short interview with Ike, Tay, and Zac and then it was time for them to perform — full force.

Even though there was room for only a few hundred fans, the noise level was high. Zac told photographer Ernie Paniccioli, "What good is it if we are a hit and we lose our hearing? Those girls should calm down a bit!"

Almost teasing Zac, the photographer pointed out, "If each girl buys a CD, you'll be well off!"

Zac snapped back, "Not if we're deaf!"

Week Two: Hanson Rules the World!
Just a few days after their *Today Show* ap-

pearance, Hanson was back on a plane, but this time they were heading for Europe to promote *Middle of Nowhere*, which was being released there on May 26. During this whirlwind trip, Ike, Tay, and Zac were stopping off in England, France, and Germany. Besides TV appearances and interviews, they were scheduled to do a major photo shoot for the American magazine *Entertainment Weekly*. London photographer Anya Grabert spent about two and a half hours with Hanson. She recalls, "They were really nice, full of energy, running around and having fun. They were very professional, but also very teenage-like — lots of good fun."

Grabert took Ike, Tay, and Zac on an outside location in London. They found some really interesting and colorful walls as backdrops, but, even though it was mid-May, it was very, very cold. "But they were very cool," Grabert jokes. "They were cooperative about it."

A typical Hanson feel surrounded the shoot — forget the hovering stylists, makeup artists, and clothing designers with their spritz and sprays, tugs and pulls, and suggestions! No, Ike, Tay, and Zac wore their *own* clothes. "That suited me," says Grabert. "I prefer them very natural. . . .They jumped around a lot and were very easygoing, very easy to work with."

During their European trip, Ike, Tay, and Zac were interviewed by the French radio station

Radio/Libre, also known as French Fun Radio. They were interviewed by reporter Florian Gazan, with the help of a translator named Lorenzo.

The interview got off to a typical start with Zac making interruptions like, ". . . . I wanna, I wanna say that. . . ." and "LET ME SPEAK!"

Florian and Lorenzo asked Ike if Zac was usually quiet and he was just acting up during the press tour! "No, no, no!" Ike laughed. "He always talks. He definitely talks. He's very animated."

When asked how they kept up with their schoolwork while promoting *Middle of Nowhere*, the boys explained that they study through a home-school program. "We take our books with us," Tay said. "Our parents just teach us. . . . Or we do it on our own. We do, actually, have a math tutor. . . . The thing is getting to travel all around — coming to Paris, going to Germany, going to London. . . . there're so many things to see. That's part of school."

They were also asked, "When a new group comes along, they're usually compared to other groups or artists — who have you been most compared to?"

"I think it's probably the Jackson 5," Ike responded. "Because their music sounds, in a lot of ways, very similar to ours. . . . The harmonies . . ."

But then interviewer Florian observed, "If we

follow the comparison to the Jackson 5, it means Zac is like the Michael Jackson of the band!"

"Eaaaaa!" screeched Zac as Florian asked, "So you intend to do plastic surgery?"

"NO! I like my face the way it is!" Zac insisted.

Back in London, the boys gave a BBC-Radio 1 interview and Taylor was asked if the rumor about his voice problems was true.

"There was this big rumor that went around that I got nodules," Tay said. Nodules are small tumorous growths that can develop on a singer's vocal cords. "[It] was in a magazine — and I'm, like, dead now. . . . I think it got dramatically exaggerated."

Throughout the interview, Zac was, as usual, very animated and was acting up. It was established early on that he got his nickname, Animal, from the Muppets character. So the interviewer asked the boys if they weren't musicians, what would they choose to be.

"I would be Zac, the . . . I don't know," Zac answered quickly.

"[Zac] the Muppet?" asked the interviewer.

"I most likely would be very calm, actually," Zac said thoughtfully.

Taylor was somewhat at a loss, saying, "I wouldn't be me if we didn't sing, you know. . . . I wouldn't know [who] I'd be if I didn't do music."

"I kinda feel the same way as Tay," Ike said.

"You know, if I was not singing, then I'd be very different because it's very much a part of me. I'd probably be doing something creative, something artistic."

"I JUST WANNA BE IN A BAND CALLED HANSON!" Zac added, getting in the last word — as usual.

The Never Ending Story

Isaac, Taylor, and Zac had been busy promoting their CD, but they kept getting busier. As the momentum built — and "MMMBop" went to the number one spot on the charts and *Middle of Nowhere* debuted at the number nine spot — Hanson returned home, at least to the U.S. They were back in New York to do more promotional interviews and appearances.

Finally, toward the end of May, the guys were able to spend a few days back in Tulsa. "It's great to be back home," Taylor said when a reporter finally found them. But there were no long, extended interviews or photo shoots. The guys just wanted to sleep in their own beds, kick a soccer ball around the yard, and spend quality time with their parents and sisters and brother.

Then, before they knew it, it was back to England to do more promotional appearances and to shoot their second video, "Where's the Love." Once again, Tamra Davis, director of "MMM-

Bop," directed. She was really glad to see the guys again. Davis had last been with the boys a couple of weeks before in L.A., but when she sat down with them to discuss their idea for this new video, she noticed that, "in the last couple of weeks, they got a little older-looking, but in a good way."

As they collaborated on their vision of the video, they kept coming back to what the song was about: images. And, once again, the four of them realized they were all thinking the same way. "What was great about that is when they came onto the set and saw they helped inspire what the set was about, they were excited," says Davis. "Like they wanted to shoot in a warehouse and when they got there, they saw it was exactly what they wanted."

Tamra was also impressed with how they were taking all their success. Since the last time she had seen them, they had hit the number one spot all over the world. But when she mentioned it, they seemed to be keeping everything in perspective. She says, "They laughed about it, saying, 'We'd be really crazy if we changed in two weeks!'"

The rest of the summer of 1997 looked as if it would be a repeat performance of the months of May and June. Hanson was scheduled to be presenters on the June 12 MTV Movie Awards, followed by live performances in Oklahoma City and Charlotte, North Carolina, and even an invitation to appear on Jay Leno's *Tonight Show*.

Mainly Ike, Taylor, and Zac were gearing up for the fall tour — and trying to keep everything in perspective. After all, Ike, Tay, and Zac were living the life they just dreamed about a year ago. Still marveling at the fact they are now MTV babies, Ike sums it all up with, "To be played on MTV as much as we're getting played is incredible. We didn't think people would think we're cool enough."

Well, Ike, you were wrong. Hanson is as cool as it gets!

"YEARBOOK SONG"

**". . . 'Cause I'm looking through the yearbook then
I find that empty space.
There's a name without a picture, but I can't
forget his face.
Tell me where did he go. I want to know.
Where did Johnny go? . . ."**

**Written by: Isaac Hanson/Taylor Hanson/Zachary
Hanson/Ellen Shipley**
Producer: Steve Lironi
Album: *Middle of Nowhere*
Length: (5:29)

FAST FACT: Isaac claims that he doesn't really have a
favorite song from *Middle of Nowhere*, that "you really get
attached to all the songs in different ways because of how
they came about or their meaning."

"Yearbook Song" — or "Johnny" as Isaac refers to it —
is the eerie song about a high school yearbook that merely
has a blank space for a boy named Johnny. "'Yearbook' is
a really cool song because of the meaning behind it," explains Isaac. "We were talking about a yearbook. . ."

". . . and a lot of times it says 'picture unavailable,'" interjects Taylor. "The song was kind of built on that
thought."

6
Tour Time

"It's a ton of fun to perform."
Isaac Hanson

Though Isaac, Taylor, and Zac spent much of the summer of 1997 making promotional appearances in the U.S. and in Europe, they were also busy making plans for a major tour in the fall of 1997. As a group Hanson admitted they enjoyed doing the various meet-and-greets with their fans, but they were really itching to get back up onstage and perform.

Shortly after their first promotional trip to Europe in May of 1997, the boys stopped off for an MTV interview and were asked about their schedule. Zac, who was a little weary from all the traveling, said, "We haven't been home for like a month." But Taylor explained, "We've basically been doing promotional stuff. We just got back from Europe, so we've been gone a lot. I guess people would want us to play. We would love to play pretty soon. It's kinda a bummer that you don't get to play all the time, but we're practicing, and hopefully, we'll tour this fall."

Ike agreed with Taylor one hundred percent! "We definitely miss performing for people. It's a ton of fun to perform!"

And what will touring be like for Hanson now? Well, Diana won't be setting up card tables, selling CDs and T-shirts, and Walker won't be carrying the equipment and tuning the guitars! But they will be there — along with Jessie, Avey, and Mackie. Some things will never change for Hanson! After three hundred gigs all across America's heartland in the past five years, the boys have the drill down pat. Of course, they will be trading in school assembly appearances for concerts at New York City's Madison Square Garden. And the audiences will number in the thousands instead of the hundreds. But that doesn't bother Hanson. Speaking for all three, Taylor exclaims, "We're not nervous at all — we can't wait to get out and do it!"

"LOOK AT YOU"

"Look at you baby
Standing in the shadows, wondering what I'm
doing here.
Wishing something would happen,
maybe I could disappear . . . ."

Written by: Isaac Hanson/Taylor Hanson/Zachary
   Hanson/Steve Lironi
Producer: Steve Lironi
Album: *Middle of Nowhere*
Length: (4:28)

FAST FACT: The lyrics of "Look at You" talk of a girl
who is something of a mystery. Hmmm, sounds a bit like
Zac! Except, of course, Zac is not a girl.

"LUCY"

**"The day that I left Lucy
A tear fell from her eye
Now I don't have nobody, and I was such a
fool. . . ."**

Written by: Isaac Hanson/Taylor Hanson/Zachary
  Hanson/Mark Hudson
Producer: Steve Lironi
Album: *Middle of Nowhere*
Length: (3:35)

FAST FACT: "I wanted to write a song with each brother," says Mark Hudson. "'Lucy' was Zac's. . . . I helped with the lyrics, but kept his perspective."

7
What the Future Holds

"We just want to keep doing our music whether we sell one record or one million."
Isaac Hanson

"I will be genuinely surprised and disappointed if the Hanson album does not turn out to be one of the biggest-selling records of 1997," Mercury Records executive Howard Berman told the *New York Post.* "If this is not a platinum album by the end of the year, I think we will have done something very wrong. This is as big a priority as any project can be, but essentially it's a self-generated thing. Hanson made themselves a priority, and the whole company is going with the flow."

And, so it seems, is the entire world. By the beginning of the summer of 1997, "MMMBop" had climbed to the number one spot in the U.S.,

England, Germany, Australia, Canada, Mexico, and even in Southeast Asia! However, no matter how solidly you are on top, there are always those who question you, those who are the voices of doom and gloom.

One doubter is *Philadelphia Inquirer* music critic Tom Moon. In his initial Hanson review of *Middle of Nowhere*, he admitted that they were a phenomenon, but he added, ". . . Unlike some other teen acts, these guys have only proven they can do one thing. It's certainly working, but you can't go to this well more than a couple of times.

"The key is, is the record company willing to let Hanson go in a different direction? Will they accept a record two years down the road that doesn't sound like this?"

Any Hanson fan will point out that's very likely. Just over the past five years, Ike, Tay, and Zac have changed from *a capella* gospel singers to R&B-influenced pop singers. And their musical and writing talent has grown by leaps and bounds with the passing of time.

David Adelson of *Hits* magazine told *USA Today* that he sees a long and rich future for Hanson. "Traditional industry naysayers would brand these guys the Top Forty flavor of the moment," he says. "However, if you look past the surface, there are quality lyrics. The record is getting critical praise."

Actually, there are many who feel that Hanson and other teen artists — such as Mercury label mates Radish, blues-guitarist/singer Jonny Lang, and rockers Savage Garden — are just the tip of the iceberg, the forerunners of a whole new kind of music. *Radio and Records* editor Tony Novia explains, "Younger audiences tend to be more passionate about music, and they tend to spend more on music. Record companies are looking at the bottom line. They are looking for the cutting edge, and I absolutely see Hanson. . . . going on to be the Next Big Thing."

There are many who agree with that point of view. As a matter of fact, some music critics have compared Hanson to the Beatles. But the brothers are not comfortable with that comparison. "You never want to say that!" Isaac wails. And Zac chimes in with, "The Beatles, I mean, they were the *Beatles*!" Summing it all up, Taylor says, "We're ladybug-size."

But what about today's pop icons? Do Ike, Taylor, and Zac see themselves wrestling the crown of King of Pop from Michael Jackson? They'll let others determine that.

"Being the 'Next Big Thing,'" laughs Zac, "it's just a good line, I guess you would say. We don't necessarily think we're the big shots."

"It's kind of a marketing thing," adds Taylor, almost embarrassed by the question. He does think that Hanson's music is coming at a good time and explains, "I think things are going away from the alternative thing. So I guess, in a way, [our music] is where music is headed. Just because the music we make is more up and just more fun."

The fact is, Hanson is having fun right now, but they are well aware that music fans' tastes can change. "I think music is always evolving, things are always changing," says Isaac. "People are always changing what they like. . . . But we've always been doing what we love to do. We weren't worrying about what other bands were doing. We do what we do and they do what they do. That's the way of the world."

And, it looks as if Hanson will be doing what they do for a long, long time to come!

"I WILL COME TO YOU"

**"... 'Cause even if we can't be together
We'll be friends now and forever
And I swear that I'll be there come what may. ..."**

**Written by: Isaac Hanson/Taylor Hanson/Zachary
Hanson/Barry Mann/Cynthia Weil**
Producer: Steve Lironi
Album: *Middle of Nowhere*
Length: (4:11)

FAST FACT: Taylor sings the lead in this song. The lyrics say that even if the love is over, the friendship doesn't have to disappear. This is a theme in many of Hanson's songs.

8
Hanson FAQs

"It's cool to have people respond to you."
Taylor Hanson

If you're a net-surfer and a Hanson fan, you've no doubt checked out the ever-growing Hanson web sites and chat rooms. There seems to be a new one every day. Here are the most frequently asked questions and answers about Isaac, Taylor, and Zac!

Q: Who is Hanson?
A: Hanson is a band consisting of three brothers, Isaac, Taylor, and Zachary. They are from Tulsa, Oklahoma, and their first major-label CD is called *Middle of Nowhere*.

Q: Does Hanson write their own songs?

A: Yes — they either wrote or co-wrote all of the songs on *Middle of Nowhere*.

Q: Does Hanson live in Los Angeles?

A: No. Their home is still in a West Tulsa suburb right outside the Tulsa city limits. However, the family did rent a house in the Hollywood Hills area of Los Angeles for six months while Isaac, Taylor, and Zac were recording *Middle of Nowhere*. Isaac says: "You could actually see the HOLLYWOOD sign from the deck on the back of the house. And you could see Mann's Chinese Theater."

Q: When was the single, "MMMBop," released?

A: March 24, 1997. It debuted at No. 49 on the *Radio and Records* chart on March 30. Six weeks later it hit the number one spot on the *Billboard* charts and stayed there for three weeks running.

Q: What are their birthdays? Is Taylor thirteen or fourteen?

A: Isaac was born on November 17, 1980; Taylor was born on March 14, 1983; Zac was born on October 22, 1985. When Hanson's record-company bio was first written, he was thirteen. His birthdate wasn't printed, so many reporters weren't aware he had turned fourteen just eight days before "MMMBop" was released!

Q: Do Isaac, Taylor, and Zac go to public school in Tulsa?
A: No, they are home-schooled and have been for years. Their mother, Diana, had been teaching them at home even before they were performing. The director of the "MMMBop" and "Where's the Love" videos, Tamra Davis, says she was impressed at how much they were into their schoolwork. "There wasn't much downtime on the set," she recalls, "but, if they weren't doing interviews, they would do schoolwork. Mostly we would just hang out and talk about stuff. A lot of times in between, I'd teach them things, like I taught them the theory of relativity and gave them a lesson on the Mars mission. We talked about Mark Twain. . . . They asked a lot of questions. They really like learning. They're very curious and really get excited about knowledge."

Q: Did Hanson use stunt doubles during the Rollerblading sequence in "MMMBop"?

A: No! It was Hanson. "The skating wipe-out was real. Definitely all real," admits Zac. (Director Tamra Davis confides, "Zac definitely falls down a lot!")

Q: Why does the car Taylor drives in the "MMMBop" video look so familiar?
A: Probably because it's the same car Sandra Bullock drives in *Speed 2*.

Q: Why is the European version of "MMMBop" different than the United States version?
A: Because of the car sequence. "We were towing the car; they're not actually driving it," says director Tamra Davis. "That's why we had so much fun with them jumping over the seat and throwing their hands in the air. . . . In Europe we had to edit that stuff out. They were like, 'We can't show kids driving recklessly.'"

Q: Is it true that Taylor cut his hair?
A: No! It was just a vicious rumor!

Q: Does Hanson have a special name for their fans?
A: Yes. They nicknamed their fans "The Scream Squad." Actually, they're amazed at all the attention they cause. "We do have

groupies," says Ike. "It's weird," adds Tay. "We kinda laugh at it, but it's cool to have people respond to you."

Q: Who sings lead on "Lucy"?
A: Zac.

Q: Is Zac Hanson the youngest artist to ever have a number one hit on *Billboard*'s Hot 100 pop chart?
A: Zac just missed that distinction by an mmmbop! He was eleven years and six months old when "MMMBop" went to number one. Michael Jackson was eleven years and five months old when "I Want You Back" earned the top spot.

Q: Is there another group that goes by the name of Hanson?
A: The Canadian group, NoMeansNo, recently did a side project album, *Sudden Death*, under the name The Hanson Brothers. The punk-music trio, who have been together since 1979, took that name in honor of the hockey-playing Hanson brothers from the 1977 Paul Newman movie *Slapshot*.

Q: Is it true that Ike, Tay, and Zac wear earplugs when they're onstage?

A: You bet! According to Zac, "We'd go deaf from all the fans screaming if we didn't!"

Q: What was Zac's first reaction when he saw "MMMBop" on MTV?
A: "I said, 'Look at the cute girl — no, wait, it's me!'" he laughs.

Q: How does Hanson describe the songs on *Middle of Nowhere*?
A: Isaac says, "There's quite a bit of variety to the songs — one makes you want to dance, it's really up and makes you feel good. And the other ones are really intense — it's like 'Wow! What's this about?' And the other ones are just mellow. We wrote every one and every one has a different meaning for us."

"A MINUTE WITHOUT YOU"

"...All the minutes in the world could never take
your place.
There's one-thousand-four-hundred-forty hours in
my day.
I've been trying to call you all day, 'cause I got so
many things that I want to say...."

Written by: Isaac Hanson/Taylor Hanson/Zachary
   Hanson/Mark Hudson
Producer: Steve Lironi
Album: *Middle of Nowhere*
Length: (3:55)

FAST FACT: Mark Hudson wrote this song with Isaac.
Hudson said it was great working with "brothers all over
again." Mark Hudson and his brothers were in the band
The Hudson Brothers in the '70s.

9
Hanson from Head to Toe

CLARKE ISAAC HANSON
Nickname: Ike
Birthday: November 17, 1980
Birthplace: Tulsa, Oklahoma
Hometown: Tulsa, Oklahoma
Parents: Walker and Diana
Siblings: Taylor, Zachary, Jessica, Avery,
   Mackenzie
Zodiac Sign: Scorpio
Hair: Blond
Eyes: Dark brown
Height: 5'10"
Musical landmark: "I actually wrote my first
   song when I was in third grade."
Instruments: Guitar, piano, vocals
Early musical influences: fifties and early six-
   ties rock and roll

Fave color: Green
Fave current music: Aerosmith, Spin Doctors,
   No Doubt, Counting Crows
Fave sports: Speed hockey, basketball
Fave Tulsa restaurant: Rex's Boneless Chicken
Fave fast food: Pizza
Fave kinds of books: Science fiction
Secret talents: Imitates Kermit the Frog, Bull-
   winkle, and Butthead; writing — he's been
   working on a sci-fi novel for a while
Self-description: "Stupid goofy"

JORDAN TAYLOR HANSON
Nickname: Tay
Birthday: March 14, 1983
Birthplace: Tulsa, Oklahoma
Hometown: Tulsa, Oklahoma
Parents: Walker and Diana
Siblings: Issac, Zachary, Jessica, Avery,
   Mackenzie
Zodiac Sign: Pisces
Hair: Blond
Eyes: Blue
Height: 5'7"
Instruments: Keyboard, bongos — lead singer
Early musical influences: Chuck Berry, Bobby
   Darin, and the Beach Boys
Fave color: Red
Fave sports: Speed hockey, basketball, soccer,
   Rollerblading

Fave pastimes: Drawing and reading
Fave fast food: McDonald's
Fave refreshment: Bottled water
Fave singers: Natalie Merchant, Alanis Morissette
Secret talent: He draws cartoon characters
Self-description: "The quiet one"
Coolest places visited: New Orleans, Los Angeles, London, New York — "We really enjoyed being in New York. We had a whole two day tour, and we walked up the Statue of Liberty."
Words to live by: "Everything changes"
Weird fact: There is a fan group on the internet called "The Taylor Hanson Cult"

ZACHARY WALKER HANSON
Nicknames: Zac; Animal (from the Muppets' character)
Birthday: October 22, 1985
Birthplace: Tulsa, Oklahoma
Hometown: Tulsa, Oklahoma
Parents: Walker and Diana
Siblings: Isaac, Taylor, Jessica, Avery, Mackenzie
Zodiac Sign: Libra
Hair: Blond
Eyes: Brown
Height: 5'3"
Instruments: Drums, vocals

Early musical influences: fifties and early sixties rock and roll

Fave singer: Alanis Morissette

Fave color: Blue

Fave sports: Rollerblading, speed hockey

Fave pastime: Drawing

Fave school subject: Math — he's a whiz kid!

Fave super heroes: Power Rangers

Fave fast food: Chicken from Rex's Boneless Chicken in Tulsa, and McDonald's (when Zac went on the early promotional tours to Europe, he was glad to see those Golden Arches down the street from Buckingham Palace and on the Champs Elysées!)

Hidden talent: He's a master skateboarder

Self-description: "The romantic one and the goofy, funny one"

WHERE & HOW TO CONTACT HANSON:

The Official Hanson Fan Club:

        HITZlist

        P.O. Box 703136

        Tulsa, OK 74170

Mercury Records Address:

        Hanson

        c/o Mercury Records

        825 Eighth Avenue

        New York, NY 10019

        or

        c/o Mercury Records

        11150 Santa Monica Blvd.

        Suite 1100

        Los Angeles, CA 90025

Hanson Management Company:

        Hanson

        c/o Triune Music Group

        8322 Livingston Way

        Los Angeles, CA 90046

Official Hanson Phone Hotline: (918) 446-3979
(Be sure to get your parents' premission!)

OFFICIAL INTERNET ACCESS
Official Hanson Web Site:
http://www.hansonhitz.com

Fan Club E-Mail Address:
http://hansonfans@hansonline.com

Mercury Records Web Site:
http://www.polygram.com/mercury/artists/
hanson/hanson_homepage.html

Ultimate Hanson Links Page:
http://www.geocities.com/Eureka/6540/

"MADELINE"

**"Out my window a memory
I'm dying inside
I know the way it should be
Even though it was right in front of me . . . ."**

Written by: Isaac Hanson/Taylor Hanson/Zachary
  Hanson/Cliff Magness
Producer: Steve Lironi
Album: *Middle of Nowhere*
Length: (4:13)

FAST FACT: There's a controversy over who "Madeline" really is, but the boys are mum on this topic.

"WITH YOU IN YOUR DREAMS"

"If I'm gone when you wake up please don't cry
And if I'm gone when you wake
up it's not good-bye
Don't look back at this time as a time of
heartbreak and distress
Remember me, remember me, 'cause
I'll be with you in your dreams...."

Written by: Isaac Hanson/Taylor Hanson/Zachary
   Hanson
Producer: Steve Lironi
Album: *Middle of Nowhere*
Length: (4:57)

FAST FACT: This song was written in memory of Jane
Nelson Lawyer, Ike, Tay, and Zac's late grandmother.

"MAN FROM MILWAUKEE
(GARAGE MIX)"

**"It started at a bus stop in the middle of nowhere
Sitting beside me was a man with no hair
From the look on his face and the size of his toes
He comes from a place that nobody knows. . . ."**

**Written by: Isaac Hanson/Taylor Hanson/Zachary
Hanson**
**Producer: The Dust Brothers (John King and
Michael Simpson)**
Album: *Middle of Nowhere*
Length: (4:57)

FAST FACT: This is a bonus cut on the CD. Its origins
are from the meanderings of Zac. "Zac was thinking about
aliens," says Isaac. "The man in 'Man From Milwaukee' is
really an alien."

But that's not all there is behind the legend. It seems
that Zac was inspired to write the song when the family
was stuck on the side of the road in their broken-down
van. They were right outside Albuquerque, New Mexico,
but Albuquerque doesn't exactly flow in the lyrics of a
song (even though the Partridge Family wrote a song
called "Point Me in the Direction of Albuquerque"). So Zac
did a little editing and changed it to Milwaukee.